ABYSSINIAN ARRANGEMENT

IRIS LEIGH

Abyssinian Arrangement

Two lucrative deals. One brokered by humans. The other negotiated by cats. All spell trouble.

My name is Kat Jones and working for cats was never part of my plan. But turns out, the cats have the last laugh because that's exactly what I do. I solve crimes in my small town.

When the local chiropractor receives a too-good-to-be-true offer to sell her practice for a life-changing amount of money, she reluctantly refuses.

Within hours, one of our own is kidnapped. Now I must team up with the office's Abyssinian cat to follow the clues and locate the missing employee before the brazen kidnapping turns deadly.

Can I solve this case before the clock runs out?

Contents

Chapter 1

"You ... again?"

I did my best to smile at his question. Mr. Higgins wasn't pleased to see me and a part of me was unsure of why I was here, but with coffee in hand he motioned me inside, a deep scowl on his face. He must know why I was here. He lifted his mug and took a long and very audible gulp. According to Mr. Higgins, it was coffee time every moment of the day.

"They are in the back. I know you two are up to something. I just don't know what."

There was a strain in his voice that I hadn't noticed when he had first opened the door. I nodded in thanks, opting to not respond. I didn't know what was going on as well, but I doubted Mr. Higgins would have taken kindly to me stating just how oblivious I was to everything.

"If you want to solve crimes, then be my guest. But my wife? She gotta stay out of it or else I'm going to go crazy! She brought up solving cases again over dinner! Dinner!" he exclaimed as he rubbed at his temples and he let out a heavy sigh. Mr. Higgins closed the door behind me as I made my way to the back. Without waiting a moment, he let loose another very audible huff as he went back to his favorite spot in the living room. The TV came alive as the show he was watching before I rudely interrupted him began playing once more. But I could feel his eyes boring holes into my back as I passed through the living room and into the kitchen and right out into the back yard. For someone who was a retired police detective, he sure wasn't subtle.

"Kat Jones! The girl of the hour!"

I slammed to a halt and furrowed my brow, taking in the scene before me. Mrs. Higgins, with a wide smile that reached from ear to ear, was sitting at one of her backyard tables. But it wasn't her that had me pausing and debating if I should turn on my heels and head home. There were several ladies of the gossip circle also situated at the table with her. None of them looked too pleased to be here, or were just unhappy with my arrival.

"Come, Kat! Come join us!"

I bit my lip, tossing a look over my shoulder at the door that would take me back inside where I could possibly make an escape. Should I do it? Surely this had to be a mistake. I thought back to the invitation made by my next-door neighbor which had prompted my arrival here on a Saturday morning at noon. She had found me soon after I had managed to ditch Lola and her Abyssinian cat friend who'd attempted to ambush me when Alec had his party.

I frowned as I looked back at the table. I had thought I was finally free of drama. But the sinking feeling in my stomach had me questioning if I'd just walked into my next case of my own free will.

"Kat, don't just stand there all day!" Mrs. Higgins exclaimed with a bubbly tone, her hand waving me closer. This was absolutely a mistake. I shouldn't have come, but my body moved forward as I made my way to the backyard table that everyone was situated at. I knew once I sat down I would be roped into whatever the gossip ring was discussing for the day. The last time I was here, Mrs. Hastings died. If I joined them today and received news that there was another death, hopefully not murder, I might just cry. Everything in this town was starting to feel like one bad dream with all the craziness.

The talking cats didn't help. They made it worse.

Under the watchful eye of Mrs. Higgins, I made my way across the small deck and to the occupied table. She gestured to the empty chair next to her like I wouldn't know where to sit. Every other chair had a body occupying it, leaving only one spot sandwiched between Mrs. Higgins and Sharon.

"Kat," Sharon said in greeting as she lifted her bubbly drink up in a cheers before taking a long chug. "Welcome to the party." She swung out her glass, motioning to the rest of the gossip ring before setting it on the table. At least I wasn't the only one not too pleased with being here today.

I slid into the empty seat as I took in the rest of the ladies at the table. Fiona West, with her long black hair braided out of her face, sat directly next to Sharon, her mouth set in a tight line, her eyes dull as she looked past Mrs. Higgins, who sat opposite of her. That pit in my stomach grew. Fiona was always the quiet one in the group, but she looked like someone had died.

"Here, have a cup of tea."

A cup was placed in front of me as Mrs. Higgins picked up the teapot to fill it up.

"Don't you think it would be better to get some alcohol in her?" This time it was Paula Gibbons who chimed in. Her and Mrs. Higgins always liked to butt head on things. Though if Paula was saying that, then I knew something bad had happened.

"Nonsense. She needs a clear mind for what we need her to do."

And there it was. A confirmation that I was being signed up for something. My gaze darted between the two women as they shot a glance at each other, the knots in my stomach tripling as I waited for more information. Whoever spoke next was going to drop a bomb on me that I wasn't prepared for. I should have made a run for it when I had the chance.

"You know what? Maybe I should just leave." I took a sip of my tea, let out a hum in delight as I proceeded to stand from my chair. "Lovely tea. I'll enjoy it next time."

"Nonsense! Like I said, you are the lady of the hour."

A firm hold on my arm prevented me from removing myself from the table. I looked at the hand wrapped around my arm to the source before letting out a sigh and sitting back down. I went back to taking in everyone at the table now that my great escape had been ruined. Next to Fiona West was Paula Gibbons, the only person who actually looked like they wanted to be here. Next to her, Doctor Charles had me wanting to scratch my head in surprise. I didn't take her as one to join the gossip ladies in their hangouts. That wasn't what I found alarming about her presence, though. It was the fact that she was the owner of a rusty orange cat—the same cat that tried to ambush me alongside Lola when Alec had his party. It seemed now that while I had successfully been able to avoid the drama the cats would have brought to me, I had not been able to avoid the humans. Whatever news was about to be shared with me had to involve Doctor Charles and the Abyssinian cat.

"Kat."

"Doctor Charles."

She had her arms crossed over her chest as she looked at me and then at Mrs. Higgins. Her body was tense. I took another sip of tea. Out of everyone here, she looked the worst. Sharon Smith looked like she had better things to be doing. Fiona West looked sad, like someone died. Paula Gibbons looked like she was going to stir the pot with drama. Mrs. Higgins looked like she was right at home. I looked like a fish out of water. But Doctor Charles? She looked like she was the one about to die.

I hoped she wasn't about to drop news that she had been poisoned and I would have to find out who did it. *Please, please, please.*

"Something happened, didn't it?" I started. "Do I even want to know?"

There was no point in avoiding it. I wasn't allowed to leave, and eventually I would be cornered by the cats of this town to work on this issue anyway. I needed to accept my fate that no matter how hard I avoided crime, it always found me, regardless of human or cat involvement. If I was able to get everything out in the air now, then I might be able to avoid the headache that came later on when being ambushed.

"Observant as always. You are really picking up on this."

There was a hint of pride in Mrs. Higgins as she smiled at me. She picked up her teacup, raising it in the air, and held it there. Understanding what she wanted, I raised my own and cheered as we nodded to each other before proceeding to take a sip. Glad I was being more observant, but it was coming too late. If I were a bit more observant in the first place, I would have just stayed home. With only a quick sip of my tea, I sat it down. I wasn't going to be distracted about why I was here. They were prolonging it for a reason, and I'd rather just rip the Band-Aid off in one go so I could hightail it far away from here.

"What is it? Just go ahead and say it."

"Well, since you ask, Ms. fancy doctor over here has gotten herself into trouble." Mrs. Gibbons jerked a thumb over to her seat buddy, who paled at the attention cast on her.

"Trouble ... that I somehow can help with?" My question came out slowly as I regretted having the Band-Aid ripped off. I wanted it to stay on and to never come off. A pang in my stomach had me picking up my tea once more, trying to distract myself. Time seemed to have slowed down, the silence becoming deafening as my lips hovered over my cup. I took a sip, and just when I was about to swallow, I had to stop to quickly beat on my chest. My simple attempt to have some tea had almost caused me to choke, all because of a few words.

"Her assistant has been kidnapped, and she got a ransom for an amount that we can't afford."

Chapter 2

They say the older you get, the higher the chance you have to go senile—that a few words could be mistaken or not heard at all. And when attempting to connect the dots, it would still be wrong. Even though I was in my late twenties, I was considering scheduling a doctor's appointment. Because obviously I needed to get my ears checked, because I did not just hear what I heard.

"You are joking, right?" I inquired, as I let loose a slight chuckle. Surely this had to be a prank. I twisted my head from side to side, trying to identify what prank was unfolding that I was the unsuspecting target for. "Did the cats put you up to this?" Another round of awkward chuckles escaped from me as I so desperately wanted all of this to be a big misunderstanding.

"What cats?"

I turned slowly to Mrs. Higgins, who had spoken, to see her looking at me with her eyebrow raised. I hadn't meant to bring up the felines that drove me crazy. It was just that usually anything crazy that happened to me had to involve them somehow. And now I was giving them more credit than I should have.

"We need your help," Mrs. Higgins continued, ignoring my comment about the cats.

My skin tingled, that heavy feeling in my stomach almost unbearable with every new word from my neighbor's mouth. Mrs. Higgins was beyond trustful, and had proved quite knowledgeable in solving other cases. I had always told her I wasn't going to make crime solving a habit, as I wanted nothing to do with it. And a kidnapping sounded like the perfect crime to draw a line in the sand and stand my ground. A person had been kidnapped and they wanted me to solve this? No way this was my life now.

"Surely you can go to the cops ... right? Like I can't be the only person you can ask for help?" My question came out shaky. I wasn't going to convince them when I couldn't even convince myself.

"It's time sensitive," Mrs. Higgins countered.

"Kidnappings usually are," I chimed in, still in a daze that this was really happening.

"There is also this," Doctor Charles said as she reached into her pocket to grab a piece a paper. She slid the folded piece of paper across the table in my direction and tapped it a few times. This looked exactly like a scene out of a movie. Time ticked away as no one reached for the piece of paper. I looked to the doctor before pointing to myself to question if I was supposed to be the one to pick it up. She nodded. Of course the paper was for me to read. With internal tears, I reached for it, and with a huge inhale, holding my breath, I opened it. Every ounce of my body screamed for me to run, to fold up the piece of paper like I hadn't just read what I did. But curiosity killed the cat.

Or more like Michael, Doctor Charles' assistant, was going to be killed.

"We know what he did. We have Michael. Pay up or he dies," I read softly, the words foreign to my tongue. This wasn't just a kidnapping. This was about to be murder. Surely I had to have read that wrong. So I read it again, and again, and about ten more times. The message on the piece of paper never changed.

This had to be a prank. Or maybe a scene in a movie? How else could I explain this note that had letters cut out of a magazine and pasted on? No one did that in the real world anymore. Those things only happened on TV. I craned my head around, trying to identify a set of cameras so I could stare into the lens and let them know this was a horrible plot. But there were no cameras, just a group of people sitting around a table with a ransom note.

"We know what he did. We have Michael. Pay up or he dies," I repeated, still unsure if I was reading it correctly. "What did he do? What does that mean?" I asked before I could bite my tongue. Curiosity was going to get me killed right alongside Michael.

"We think they are talking about his money issues," Mrs. Higgins said before picking up her cup of tea to take a sip. She acted like we were discussing the weather, and maybe to her it was. Certainly not to me though—this was absolute craziness. She turned to the doctor for a moment before settling her gaze on me once more. "All we know is he got into some money issues. Doctor Charles, being a kind boss and friend, paid it off in order to keep him away from the loan sharks who threatened to remove a body part or two."

I reeled back in my seat, almost sending myself tumbling down to the ground. "We have crazy loan sharks in town too?" I squeaked. It was official. I needed to pack my bags and get out-of-town, fast. I had once thought I lived in a nice, quiet, cozy town where nothing happened. That was a severe understatement. It was crime after crime. And now this?

"I don't..." I started to protest to somehow plead my case but Mrs. Higgins butted in, sensing my hesitation as I set the letter down on the table.

"It won't be too dangerous if the case is solved in four days."

"Why is that?" There I went again, talking before thinking. I wanted to slap myself in the face for how foolish I was being. I needed to seal my lips so they could never utter another word.

"According to the brick the letter was attached to, that is all we have."

"There was a brick too?"

"So four days. All of this just happened today?"

"Ah no." Mrs. Higgins smiled. "Started two days ago. It's a bit hard to solve cases with the husband about."

Doing the mental math of the information provided, I asked, "So two days, then?"

"No, four days. We had a week. Doctor Charles over here thought it was a joke at first, so she delayed with telling me. Then I attempted to solve it and now we are here." She waved about the table as if what she said was so casual. That being kidnapped for three days and there were only four days left was a normal thing. I let loose a groan. It was much worse than I expected.

"There is more," Doctor Charles piped in.

"There always is," I softly grumbled under my breath as I turned to focus on the lady who had arrived with the note. Her body was still tense as she stared at me. I guess if I knew my assistant had been kidnapped, and it was all up to me to fork over money I didn't have, then I would be stressed too. After all, who just had a huge lump sum of money sitting around for a rainy day? Actually...

"Wait. Did you ask Alec? I mean, he has billions. I'm sure he can afford to give some away."

"I'm disappointed in you, Kat. You never pay ransoms."

I looked over at Mrs. Higgins, who had spoken, raising my eyebrow. She obviously didn't know me too well, because I would pay that ransom if I had the money.

"Tell Kat about your offer."

Doctor Charles nodded and she leaned forward, her voice slightly lower than before. The only people outside were us girls at the table, so I wasn't sure why she was speaking so softly.

"Michael asked to borrow some money to pay off the guys he got in trouble with." I nodded. I already knew that part of the story. The loan sharks that probably had no problem with chopping a few fingers, maybe even a leg, or hand...

I shuddered at the thought.

"But a few days after, I got an offer for my practice."

Now that was a new piece of information. Doctor Charles owned Cracking Chiropractic, the only chiropractic office in town. But where was she going with this? Were the two related? Needing something to help soothe my nerves, I picked up my cup of tea once more and took a quick sip. It didn't have the same impact as before, as now it was growing warm from being exposed to the elements.

"Sell my practice for a million dollars."

I banged on my chest, trying to stop the choking. Everything was traveling down the wrong pipe today.

"Millions?" I somehow managed to croak out.

"Single million, just a million."

Millions. Million. All the same things in my book. It was way more money than I would ever be able to touch.

"Did you accept it?" I asked, leaning in closer, fully invested in the conversation now that I had fixed my choking situation.

"No. Sometimes, when an offer is too good to be true, you shouldn't accept."

Unless it involves millions, or in Alec's case, billions. Alec had been given a house with an inheritance of billions for just being a nice person. That was more of a too-good-to-be-true situation than this. This one had an exchange, a business for money. Was the business worth a million dollars?

"To pay the ransom, I would need to finalize the deal, but I just can't. This is my life, the only thing I have."

And Michael was going to be six feet in the ground because of it, but I kept that comment to myself. No reason to pour salt into the wound that could be healed with a million dollars.

"Don't worry, Kat will look into it."

I quickly whipped my head to the side to look at my neighbor, who was starting to gain a habit of signing me up for stuff. There must be something about me that screamed I was for hire. First, the cats thought I could be bossed around to solve crimes for them in exchange for nothing. And now we were adding humans to the mix? I couldn't figure out what was worse: having the ability to talk to cats, a feline who thought she was my boss, or going after a kidnapper who wasn't above committing murder.

Quickly weighing the pros and cons of the two, one was long term for all that I knew. I had yet to find a way to get the talking cats to stop. The other was short term. If I solved the case, it would be done, and if I didn't, I was going to be done regardless because Michael would be dead. I crinkled my nose as I sighed. It was a tie in my book.

Chapter 3

When presented the chance to escape the gossip ring before they could drop any more bombs on me, I took it. I seized the moment to wave goodbye to Mr. Higgins and run out their front door. Now all I had to do was make it safely inside my home and things might just be alright.

Which might not be happening—a spot up ahead was growing in size as it bounced down the street. A small little thing with a tail in the air. A deep sigh escaped me as I slouched. It didn't take a genius to guess who it was. She walked like she had no fear, that she ruled the street. If I were being honest to myself, she ruled my life. I finished walking the short distance from Mrs. Higgins' home to my own, then quickly stuffed the key inside the lock and opened the door for the cat that was taking its sweet time.

"Finally, I have been trying to talk to you."

"About my car warranty?" I absentmindedly replied to the feline.

"Huh? What are you talking about?"

I looked down at the little feline stood right outside the front door, not yet stepping through the threshold of my home. Her tail twitched behind her as she held my gaze.

"Sorry, thought you were someone else for a moment. Welcome back, Lola."

"How could you mistake me for someone else?"

A deep sigh escaped. "You missed the whole point..." I muttered as I walked into the house. Lola quickly followed into the house. I shut the door and locked it, and on autopilot, I made my way over to the kitchen.

"Dinner?" Luna asked when she quickly ran into the kitchen as I opened a can.

"Dinner," I replied as I quickly got to work on feeding them their wet cat food. Grabbing the small bowls I used for their food, I got to work portioning their meal. Before giving them their food, I headed to the fridge to grab food for myself. Leftovers, to be exact. A chicken burrito bowl that I popped into the microwave to heat up while I picked up their plates and placed them on the floor for them. All the cats, including Zaira, dived into their wet cat food.

The microwaved dinged and I grabbed my bowl along with a spoon before heading over to the couch. After today, all I wanted was some good food and to relax.

"We need to talk," Lola piped up as she followed me and jumped onto the couch. I didn't answer her as I clicked on the TV. Hopefully, she would get the message I was absolutely spent and didn't have any energy to get bossed around by a cat.

She didn't. I glanced at the light pressure she applied to my arm.

"Can I help you? I already fed you. Now it's time I feed myself."

Lola tapped my arm once more. "We got some big trouble."

"We? You mean you and not we, right?" I countered.

"No, I spoke correctly. We got trouble."

"Let me guess, it involves the chiropractor's cat."

"Finally, you are becoming more observant, thank goodness! That will help expedite our future cases!"

"It was hard not to make the connection. You did show up to my house with the cat."

"Wait!" Lola squeaked out beside me. "You saw us and didn't come home?"

Ah, I had made a mistake again. I was starting to develop a habit of letting tidbits of information slip that were better kept to myself. I needed to bite my tongue more.

"I thought it was just human bad eyesight," she mumbled to herself before shaking her head. "Regardless of what happened, you can't delay the inevitable! The case has been accepted and I'm tasking you to solve it.

"And let me guess," I started as I shoved a spoonful of my chicken burrito bowl in my mouth before continuing to speak. "Got to solve a kidnapping case, right?"

"Kidnapping? What are you talking about?"

The next spoonful of chicken didn't make it to my mouth as I turned to the feline next to me and I raised my eyebrows and spoke in disbelief: "You don't know about the kidnapping?

"What? No! I don't know anything about a kidnapping. You were hired to look into Michael. Ambrose said he had gotten into some trouble and was dragging the doctor into it."

"Ah. Well, you are late with the news. Turns out he had money problems, Doctor Charles paid it, and now Michael has been kidnapped. All of it will end in four days with him either returned or six feet in the ground if his ransom doesn't get paid. Well..." I paused as I looked at the TV to see the time. "Less than four days, because most of today is gone. Maybe like seventy-five hours or so? But who is really counting?" I shoved another bite of my chicken bowl in my mouth.

"It seems this case is more dire than I had thought." Lola jumped off the couch, not making a single sound as she landed on the floor. "I will need to charge an extra fee for the extra work."

That was it.

"HELLO, ARE YOU EVEN LISTENING TO ME?" I hollered as my body shook on the couch. "Someone has been kidnapped, and they want money to be forked over. Money nobody has, except Alec, but he doesn't count—nevertheless, no one has the money to pay the ransom. Do you?" I asked as I jabbed my spoon in Lola's direction.

"I have no need for human currency."

"Of course you don't, you are a cat. A talking cat that accepts cases and forces this human..." I poked myself with the spoon for extra emphasis so she knew exactly who we were talking about. "...to solve them. This guy is about to get murdered! M-U-R-D-E-R-E-D, which is six feet in the ground if you didn't know! I could end up dead if I work this case, which means no one would be around to feed you." I grumbled as I shoved a spoonful of food in my mouth. I needed my comfort food or I was going to blow a gasket.

"Cats are resourceful when it comes to finding meals."

"Thanks ... thanks for letting me know I can be thrown away."

"Regardless, the case has been accepted, which means it must be solved. While you work on that, I will be working on collecting the extra fee." Lola walked off towards the front door hollering back as she did so: "Open the front door. I got business to take care of."

My body moved on autopilot, setting the bowl down on the couch as I got up to let the bossy cat outside. Lola was the leader, and I was just a simple human who followed orders even if it had me going after someone who had no problem committing murder, because there was no way I was going to be solving this case in such a time crunch.

With the door closed behind her, I took a moment to breathe. I would finish my food, watch a bit of TV, and just relax. Tomorrow would be a new day and I could figure out what to do about this case that both humans and cats wanted me to solve.

"This is good!"

I frowned as I turned back towards the living room. Luna had jumped up on the couch and helped herself to my bowl of food. The one I had only managed to have a few bites of.

"I'm glad one of us could enjoy it," I grumbled.

What a day.

#

Chapter 4

I stared at Cracking Chiropractor's sign for a moment. I was really doing this. The lobby was empty save for a rusty orange cat staring at me. Of course she would be here. She lived here. Other than the four-legged feline, there was no human in sight, but Doctor Charles was probably in the back room. Letting loose a sigh, I pushed open the door and entered the business.

"Hello."

"Finally! If I had known you would be this late, I would have hired someone else."

I stared at the rusty orange feline as I mulled over her words. Why were all cats so bossy?

"Late? I didn't set an appointment with you. Also, if you could hire someone else, then please do so. It would save me a headache." For added measure, I rubbed at my temples as I stared into the cat's yellow eyes as she wrapped her tail around her paws and sat quietly.

"Exactly..." I mumbled. "I'm just here to collect some clues. You wanted me to look into Michael. Why?" I questioned as I looked around the shop to see if anything was broken. Or blood. Did the kidnapping happen here, or did it occur somewhere else? I let loose another sigh. I really had no idea how to solve this.

"He has been running my owner dry of her money! She even had to downgrade my food! A girl has got to keep her coat looking good, and only the best quality of food will do."

Of course that was the reason I was here. It was always about the food. Food this, food that. Never for the good of a human did they ask me to put my life on the line. But what was to be expected? Food was a good motivator. Despite the good motivator, I did give her an eye roll.

"Yes, he got himself into some trouble, which required him to get bailed out by your owner." I waved at the cat, dismissing the situation. "Everyone gets into trouble now and then."

"Does it typically involve drugs?"

My mind screeched to a halt. Squinting, I leaned towards the feline. But she didn't take back what she said. She had meant that Michael had somehow gotten himself mixed up with drugs. We had someone who kidnapped and was willing to commit murder. Then we couldn't forget the loan sharks who had no issues causing bodily harm. Did that mean there was a type of drug trafficking unfolding in town as well? I sighed as I tapped my fingers against my chin. All of this was starting to sound exactly like a movie and not real life.

"What exactly did you hear about the drugs?" I questioned the cat as I made my way over to sit in one of the chairs in the waiting room.

"Not much. Just that he used to use them. I believe at one point he had mentioned a deal with the dealers, but I only caught the tail of his conversation."

"Seems you heard an awful lot."

"Yes, it doesn't help when there is only you about who can hear me, and you like to show up late."

I knew her words were supposed to be taken as an insult, but I let it pass. Only this one time, though. The cats couldn't keep getting away with insulting the only help around.

"Is your owner here? I need to look around the place." Thinking back to the advice Mrs. Higgins gave me about how to solve a crime, I said, "I need to establish my crime scene." All the advice Mrs. Higgins had given me did make my job easier. I looked around the office, taking in the room. I stood and made my way over to the receptionist's desk as I remembered first meeting Michael. He hadn't talked much, but he had seemed like an alright guy. We probably wouldn't have been friends, but I didn't think he was bad enough to have all this happen to him, especially being kidnapped. But if drugs were involved, then that could explain some of the craziness unfolding in town.

I looked at the computer setup on the desk, and with a simple crack of my fingers I got to work trying to see if I could glean anything from the device. He had been kidnapped a few days ago. It would be a good start to see if there was anyone else here on that day. Maybe they saw something that could be helpful in determining if it was the loan sharks or the people connected with the drugs. Names upon names flashed on the screen as I maneuvered to the correct day— three days ago—when he had last been seen. The printer roared to life as I printed out a list. Hopefully, the doctor didn't mind that I had invited myself to her information.

"How long will it take for you to solve this?"

"Considering there is a time limit on the case, it's going to get solved one way or another." Either Michael would make it back home safely, or he would be six feet in the ground. "It doesn't help if you are going to be nagging me the whole time."

I stood to rummage in the cabinets by the desk. A feeling of familiarity washed over me. Crime solving was starting to become second nature, and that wasn't a good thing. I needed to solve this case as soon as possible. Then I could nip this crime solving in the bud.

Cracking open the filing cabinet, I looked at the little tabs as I thumbed through the manila folders, trying to see if anything stood out to me. The far back folders were dated too far in the past to be of relevance, unless this was a long con, which I doubted. Mrs. Higgins had pointed out Michael was new in town. Instead, I focused on the most recent ones, closer to the cabinet door. Quickly removing them and closing the cabinet door behind me with my side, I sat back down at the desk.

The first folder wasn't of much use, just a bunch of bills. The next folder I opened contained a bunch of medical jargon that I had no skills to read or attempt to decipher. Hopefully, it wouldn't be important. I closed that folder and set it on top of the bills folder. It wasn't until the third folder that I saw the purchase offer for the Cracking Chiropractic. Now this was useful. This was the offer they had provided to the doctor for her to sell her practice. The money, which was bold on the piece of paper that contained many zeros, had me letting loose a whistle in appreciation. She hadn't been kidding when she talked about being offered a million dollars for her practice.

"Are you done over there yet?"

I popped my head over the counter to look at Ambrose, who had jumped up on the counter to peer down at me. Again, another sigh escaped from my lips. Hadn't I basically told her to let me work?

"You know it takes some time to look into things? Things just don't magically unfold in front of me."

"Well, you have a time limit. Should you be sitting and doing nothing?"

I sighed—I was doing a lot of that lately—as I lifted the papers in the air, waving them in the cat's face. "I'm not just sitting doing nothing, I'm trying to work."

"Kat, who are you talking to?"

My head whipped around so fast that a shock vibrated through my neck. The doctor was standing there.

"Just talking to myself," I mumbled. It was the best answer I could come up with since I couldn't say I was talking to her very bossy cat.

"Are you okay? Are you sane enough to be helping me on this case?"

Was this my time to plead insanity so I could get out of it? Would she really accept it if I tried to weasel my way out? Even if she did, Mrs. Higgins wouldn't, and I didn't want her to be disappointed in me, so I sucked it up and just smiled. Doctor Charles leaned over to grab the papers from me, and she ruffled through them to see what I had been looking over.

"I see you found the offer without needing prompting on where to find it."

"I figured since I was hired I could just help myself to the information."

"Come to the back so we can talk. I'm going to close up for the day. It's hard to work with everything going on."

Doctor Charles shifted away, giving Ambrose a quick pat before she walked to the back of the building. With a quick glare in the rusty cat's direction, I picked up my papers and followed. And just like that, I was working my fourth case. I paused momentarily as I realized this was my fourth case! No wonder everyone thought I was out here solving cases like it was my job.

Chapter 5

My feet almost touched the ground as I sat on the bed in the small room we had gone into. I had thought we were going to an office that was located in the back, but instead it was just an exam room, where she no doubt cracked some backs—and where there was a creepy skeleton situated in the corner staring at us. Doctor Charles paid the skeleton no mind as she sat down on a stool before sliding over to grab the papers from my hands once more.

"Did you have a chance to read all of this?"

"Not yet. I got distracted."

I didn't elaborate on what had distracted me. More like what four-legged feline kept trying to poke jabs at me. Honestly, Ambrose was on par with being just as impatient as Lola, and that was a hard thing to do.

"There is a clause to the buyout in order for it to go through."

"A clause?" I inquired as I took the papers back from the doctor to see what this additional request was.

"I told you a too-good-to-be-true offer. It's too good to be true."

"I mean a million dollars to buy your practice is already crazy, but it sounds like a good deal. You can just buy another spot in town."

"I can't," Doctor Charles said. "They just don't want my practice for a million dollars. They want me as well."

"Want you in what way? I'm pretty sure you can't buy humans anymore, unless we traveled back in time," I muttered as I looked at the purchase letter in confusion. Did they really put a price tag on a human?

"Kat, seriously? Not in that way! They want to buy Cracking Chiropractic but still have me be the figurehead and still work here.

"Oh, sorry ... if you are still going to work here and it's still going to be a chiropractic office, why are they buying it? For a million dollars too."

This was a too-good-to-be-true offer. A million dollars to tear down the building and do something else made sense. But a million dollars to buy something and not make a single change was crazy. Too crazy to believe.

"Too good to be true, like I said."

"It does sound like that..." I pursed my lips, wondering how to say my next words without it sounding bad. "Not to be mean. I honestly just don't know. But is your business really worth a million dollars? Like ... do you have that much in sales or something?

The doctor grimaced as she crossed her arms over her chest. With a huge sigh, she answered, which I already kind of knew the answer to. This was a small town, after all. "Not even close."

I nodded slowly. Yup, it was too good of an offer, and now it was an extreme red flag. I raised my eyebrows as I tilted my head to the side. Surely there was something going on and I was just oblivious to it.

"Did they say why they wanted to buy your practice?"

"No, just received the offer, and that's it."

"That's it? Seriously…"

"Yes … well actually no," the doctor said while she stood from her seat and paced around the exam room. She stuffed her hands into the pockets of her white lab coat. I could tell she was beyond anxious. Who wouldn't be in her situation?

"What else happened?" I inquired.

"They called at first with a lower offer, but I thought it was a prank so I hung up." She stopped pacing as she looked at me. Her eyes were heavy as she kicked at the floor. "Then they kept calling, and the letter arrived. The deal is sweeter than before."

"The million dollars and buying you," I finished her train of thought. She nodded, indicating I had nailed it on the head. I couldn't help but bite the inside of my lip as I looked over the papers once more.

"And the offer was just out of the blue? You weren't trying to sell your practice, correct?"

"No, that is what's weird. I had given Michael all of my money to get him out of trouble. I hadn't even been late on a bill yet to trigger any kind of delinquent notifications, and yet two weeks after paying out they were calling."

I thought over her story before voicing what I thought might be happening.

"Maybe they are in league with the people Michael owns money to?" I asked. After all, how else would they know she had used up all her money? "Did you talk to the people Michael owed before paying them?"

"I did a few times. They had wanted the money in twenty-four hours, but I told them that it was impossible. I needed more time to gather all the funds."

"And how much money did you give to the loan sharks?" I asked

"I gave them $150,000."

My mouth dropped. Somehow I managed to close it to speak: "That's $150,000 to the loan sharks, and yet you receive an offer for a million bucks? Something really isn't adding up."

I looked at Doctor Charles for a moment, pondering over if I really wanted to ask my next question. In order to solve a crime, clues had to be connected which would lead to the culprit. There had to be some type of connection, but yet nothing was standing out except for one thing. The doctor hadn't wanted to sell her business, and she also didn't have prior interactions with the loan sharks.

"Do you think ... Michael was involved?" It was a horrible thing to think, but everything was so bizarre.

"Impossible. He is too sweet."

Well, just because the doctor thought it was impossible for him to be involved, I added him to my suspect list. Mrs. Higgins always said not to rule out anyone—*everyone is a suspect till the case has been closed.*

"Thanks for the information. I should get back to looking into this. Time limit and all."

"Before you go..." Doctor Charles reached into the pocket of her pants, withdrawing a crumpled business card, and handed it to me. "Here."

"A number?" I asked, as I smoothed out the card and stared at the number that had been scribbled on it.

"To the loan sharks. You can take the buyout papers as well."

I stuffed the loan shark's number into the manila folder that contained the buy-out papers so I wouldn't lose this important information. With a nod, I left the room. Doctor Charles opted to stay behind.

"Did you figure out the case?" Ambrose asked from her position on one of the chairs in the lobby as I made my way to leave the office.

"Hopefully soon..."

Chapter 6

"One iced coffee with a double shot of espresso," Daniel said as he leaned over the counter, sliding the cup of coffee into my waiting hands. I should have been out and about trying to solve the case, but I still needed to make a connection of how everything fit together. Getting some extra fuel with a double shot was sure to jumpstart my brain. And there was only one cafe that came to mind: Sips of Temptation.

"Thanks," I muttered as I consumed a large gulp of the iced coffee. Time was of the essence after all, and the sooner the two shots of espresso went to work the better.

"We have a new hire," Daniel chimed as he motioned to the lady behind the counter with him. I had noticed her, but I wasn't sure if she was new or not. I looked at the girl as I tilted my head. She had the same color of red hair as Sharon Smith.

"Is she related to Sharon?" I inquired as I took another large gulp of my iced coffee.

"Just because she has red hair doesn't mean they are related," Daniel said with mirth in his tone. I raised an eyebrow. "But yes, they are related. Belle is her niece."

"Nice to know." I waved the manila folder in Daniel's face as I walked away. "Got a case to solve!"

It was time to focus. I slid into an empty seat at a table. I had only just managed to open the folder before Daniel bounced over with his own drink in hand and a big smile on his face.

"Do you need some help?"

Without waiting for an answer, Daniel sat down at the other empty chair and waited.

"If you can make dots connect off of utter gibberish, then sure, please be my guest." I motioned to the folder as Daniel scooted his seat closer to me, almost pressing his chair against mine so he could peer at the contents. I pushed the papers his way so he would have an easier chance of reading it.

There had to be something here that I wasn't seeing. A set of eyes that belonged to a person who had nothing to do with this might be able to see something I didn't. Would Daniel be able to uncover a crucial piece of information? Maybe he would be able to find out why someone wanted to spend a million dollars and why Michael had to be kidnapped. I ruffled through several pages myself while Daniel looked over a few himself. All of it was just legal jargon upon legal jargon, which all went over my head.

"Have you tried calling them?"

"Calling who?" I asked as I reviewed the piece of paper before taking a sip of my iced coffee.

"The phone number on the paper," Daniel asked. He picked up the business card that Doctor Charles had handed me and pointed to the messy handwriting. I snorted before answering him.

"Yes, because calling a loan shark that is willing to maim someone sounds like a splendid idea."

"Wait ... what?"

I set my coffee on the table. I had done it again. Accidentally blurting out too much information. I took in Daniel's wide eyes, raised eyebrows, and slightly open mouth, and understood he was shocked. That had made two of us when I had found out the information as well. At least someone else was along for this crazy ride. Just wait till he found out Michael might actually end up dead, and we had a time limit to solve all of this. It was a lot of pressure to put on a person. I took another sip of my iced coffee.

"Are you in trouble?"

"Thankfully, I'm not. There is absolutely no need to worry about what I just said. All of it was a simple slip of the tongue."

I quickly tried to gather the papers together in order to hide the full contents of what exactly was going on. No reason to drag others into this crazy nonsense. It was already bad enough that I had been dragged in.

"I don't mind helping," he said as he scratched at the back of his neck. "I just don't want to end up missing a leg, or an arm, or dead..." he jokingly said as he let loose a small laugh. Daniel reached for my folder, pulling the papers back.

Well, having some extra help would be nice.

"Okay, but you can't talk to others about this."

"I don't think anyone would believe me anyway."

I leaned into Daniel as I took another sip of my iced coffee. He had volunteered himself to join this wild ride, and once he was on it there was no turning back. I knew this firsthand. So with no time to waste as we were against the clock, I spilled everything to him.

It was satisfying to watch his face morph into every emotion possible as I told him everything I had so far. Was this what I looked like when the gossip ring had spilled the news to me? Daniel's eyebrows knitted together, lips pursed as if not believing what I said. Only for his mouth to drop lower and lower as I neared the end. I had to give him credit; he didn't interrupt, just nodded every so often to indicate he was listening.

"So, are we going to call them, then?"

"Are you serious—after everything I just said?" I countered.

"Well, why not? How else are we going to figure this out?"

I mulled over his words. He had a point. It would be easier to gather information if it came right from the source. "I guess." I groaned as I picked up the business card that had the loan shark's number. Within a moment, I had dug into my pocket and removed my cell phone. Giving it no thought, I punched in the number and held the device up to my ear.

"Put it on speaker," Daniel whispered as he elbowed me in the side.

"Others might hear," I countered, and he nodded in reply, only to press his cheek to my cheek as I held the device between our ears. My face heated at the close contact and I could see others in the cafe shooting us a look before going back to enjoying their drinks and food.

"Hello," a deep, gruff voice said once the dial tone stopped ringing.

"Hi! This is … uh…" I looked over at Daniel as I stumbled on how to introduce myself. Surely I couldn't use my real name. That was a very bad idea. Especially since they were okay with causing bodily harm. I didn't need them just showing up at my front door. I glanced around the cafe, trying to come up with a plausible name that wouldn't be too hard to remember. The bell over the cafe door jingled, and walking in, posed like a boss, was Sharon.

"Sharon," I blurted, "My name is Sharon."

Daniel let out a small chuckle as I elbowed him in the side to get him to quiet down. If he didn't lower his voice soon, than the people on the phone would be able to hear him.

"What can I do for you, Sharon?" The gruff voice was back as he grumbled out his question. Just hearing the man speak made my ear tingle. He didn't sound like someone people crossed, or if they did they didn't live long to tell the tale. I gulped, swallowing some of my nervousness as I forced myself to speak.

"Who am I speaking to?" I inquired, trying to keep my voice steady, so I didn't sound scared out of my mind.

"What can I do for you, Sharon?" he repeated, causing me to bite the inside of my cheek to physically stop myself from letting out a whine. This was going to be a lot harder than I expected. It was like trying to squeeze information out a brick wall. Definitely this man was someone not to mess with and here I was trying to do that.

"Right. I was just wondering about your services."

"What services would that be, Sharon?"

Daniel pulled away from me for a moment so he could look into my eyes. His eyes were wide, and he was shaking his head no. He was alarmed by how the phone call was going. That made two of us.

The man on the other end was in control, not letting a single piece of information slip past him. Somehow, I needed to find a way to flip the switch, so I was in control

"Why don't you run me through what you offer?" I curled my lips into a small grin, satisfied that I may have finally gotten him right where I wanted him.

"Goodbye, Sharon."

An audible beep pulled me out of my victory dance in my mind as I stared at my phone. The man had ended the call just like that.

Absolutely no information had been gained from him. The only thing I confirmed was he was not someone to mess with.

"No way he did that…" I muttered as I quickly hit the redial button on my phone. It only rang for a moment before the line went dead. "He just declined my call…"

"Call the next number," Daniel said as he slid another piece of paper in front of me.

"What number?" I asked as I looked down to see who our next target was going to be.

Daniel pointed to the letter from the people who wanted to buy the chiropractor's office. Clearly written on the paper was the info of the company that had sent the offer.

Oh, that number.

"ABC Realtor Group. This is Adam."

"Hi there, this is Sharon."

The man on the other end had a chipper high-pitched tone than the loan shark, but he did sound like he wanted the day over. At least he sounded nicer than the other guy. Hopefully, I would be able to gleam some information from him.

"What can I do for you, Sharon?"

"I was wondering about your services."

"Services? In regards to what?"

"Could you tell me about your services?"

"Ma'am, our services aren't open to the public. Are you with a group we have partnered with? If so, let me know the group number and I would be more than happy to provide you services we are able to offer for your select group. If you aren't part of a group, then I am sorry, but I will not be able to offer any help."

"I'm sorry I can't remember the group number, but we recently received an offer from you," I replied, hoping that I would be able to wiggle myself in to get his help.

"Oh, I'm sorry!" Adam enthusiastically replied. "Why didn't you say that earlier? What is your establishment called? I'll pull it right up!"

I relayed the name of Doctor Charles' workplace. I could hear the clicking of his keyboard as he searched his database.

"Ah yes! Cracking Chiropractic! What a fine establishment. Are you calling to accept our offer?"

"Actually, can you tell me more about your offer? I don't remember all the details and I just want to make sure I have my notes right."

Daniel next to me gave me a thumbs-up as he continued to press his cheek against me. I wish I would have brought headphones so we didn't look we were up to no good.

"Absolutely! Give me one moment, Sharon, to pull up the rest of your file."

Adam's fingers strummed against his keyboard once more, filling the line with his clicky keyboard. There was a pause of his keyboard before it came back at a faster pace.

"What is your last name, Sharon?" he inquired.

Without thinking, I blurted out the first thing that popped into my mind. A very basic but common name. "Jones. Sharon Jones."

"Hmm ... Sharon Jones ... I don't see a Sharon Jones on record. To confirm you own the practice?" Adam's question had me pausing, biting my lip as I looked to Daniel. There was no way I could lie about that. That could get me into some deep water. Daniel shrugged, providing no help on how to answer the man's question, who waited on the line with absolute silence, no clicking of his keyboard to fill the space.

"Not exactly…" I started. "I work there."

"Well, Sharon Jones, I'm sorry, but I can only discuss the details of this offer with the owner. If you are not the owner, than I will not be able to offer my services." The man's tone quickly changed to lose some of his enthusiasm now that he'd identified I wasn't a client.

"Do you guys have a local office? Maybe I can stop by the with my boss?"

It was a shot in the dark to try and glean more information from Adam. If I could get to see him face to face, then it would be harder to turn me away. Unlike the loan shark, who had no problem promptly hanging up on me.

"We are not. We are located in Chicago."

I couldn't help but squish my eyebrows together and blow out my cheeks while I thought over his words. If they were involved with what happened with Michael, then someone had to be here. But they were located in Chicago. It would be the perfect alibi to make it seem like it wasn't them if they were saying they were based out of state and didn't have a local office.

"Oh … so there is no one in town I can talk to?"

"No." His response was curt, no fluff added to it like his response like before to make it sound more polite. Before I had a chance to question him, a sense of déjà vu washed over me as there was an audible click and the phone went silent. Daniel pulled away from me as I looked at my phone.

"He hung up."

"Think he's on to us?" Daniel asked.

"Possibly … but if they aren't located here, did they really have anything to do with this?" I paused as I thought about everything that unfolded. "But then why hang up so quickly when I asked if anyone was in town? Something is off."

"Someone could be in town—like a hitman! If they got millions to throw on an offer, then surely they have enough to hire a hitman to do their dirty work."

I looked over to Daniel as I processed his suggestion. It would have been farfetched what he had said if Michael wasn't already missing and a ransom letter wasn't received. Compared to everything else, it didn't seem that unbelievable. It actually fit right in with this crazy town. This case just kept getting weirder and wilder. Every moment, I found out something new to the point that talking cats sounded normal.

Chapter 7

Daniel pushed his chair back over to the other side of the cafe table we shared. Now all we had to review was the paper on the table and the limited amount of information we were able to glean from Adam. A few hours after our phone call with the people, we were still in the same exact spot, unable to fully connect the dots.

"You think the doctor should just accept the offer?" Daniel asked as he sipped on his refill.

"Worst case scenario, she probably will. It's one thing to sell your business, but to also work for them? That was a loss of freedom she hadn't anticipated.

"A million dollars though ... that's a lot," Daniel butted in as he pointed to the letter that had the offer amount in bold on it.

"Are you Kat Jones?"

I looked up at the mention of my name from a voice I didn't recognize. I certainly didn't recognize the man standing at the edge of the table. One of his hands was tucked into the pocket of his black slacks and the other clutching his black leather briefcase. He wore a black suit jacket over his white-button shirt and a simple black tie. It wasn't hard to tell he was a businessman by how he wore a suit and carried a briefcase, but why was here? He popped his suitcase on the table and I hoped that my prayers had been heard and there was a large sum of money in there that he was going to give me, but there had to be a catch. There was always a catch.

"It depends. Why?" I responded, knowing my response would identify me as the person he was searching for. As I shifted in my seat, I got a better look at the man that was either going to make or break my day. His hair was kept short, deep dark circles underneath his eyes showed that this man didn't know what a good night of rest meant. Then there was the vacant look on his face and I shivered. He was going to break my day. I just wanted some good luck for once in my life, not more bad stuff.

"Are you Kat Jones?"

I sighed. What was with people repeating their questions over and over today?

"Yes, I am," I replied, already getting ready to have a bomb dropped on me. The man nodded as he clicked open his briefcase. I leaned over to try to peer at the contents, a little part of me hoping there would still be money involved. But all the man did was scoot the briefcase closer to the edge so I couldn't peer inside without me tumbling over from my seat.

Quickly, he riffled around, pulled out a large envelope, and slammed his briefcase closed, locking it in the process. He handed it out to me. I looked at him before hesitantly reaching for the offering.

"What's this?" I asked as I opened up the envelope and started to pull out the documents.

"A cease-and-desist letter."

"Huh? For what? I haven't done anything."

Or at least I thought I hadn't done anything. Had the cats done something, and they were able to link it back to me? Someone cleared their throat, and I looked up from the papers filled with legal jargon to see Daniel staring at me. I had forgotten he was here for a moment.

"I have been hired to represent ABC Realtor Group. If you continue to harass my client, then I will be forced to press charges."

"Harass? I don't think giving them a phone call and inquiring what services they offered can be considered harassment."

"They are aware of who you are and what you do. If you continue to harass them, then I will go for the highest punishment the law allows.

"Court? What are you talking about?" I waved the paperwork in the air as I stood and looked at the man, holding his gaze. "What are you on? I haven't done anything, and what do you mean you are aware of who I am and what I do?" I squinted as I jabbed him with the paperwork. "Are you a stalker? How did you even find me?"

"Caller ID."

Oh.

I stopped glaring at the man as I sat back down in my seat. That actually made perfect sense. Of course, when I called the company they would be able to tell who had called them with caller ID. A few quick searches and they could find more information about me on the internet. I froze. He said he knew who I was and what I did? What did I do for him to be so alarmed? Was there some type of rumor going around on the internet about me that I didn't know about?

"I will be watching you. If you bring up my client in any way and cause bad press, I will know."

"All this because of a phone call? That is suspicious. A big red flag, I say. Who are you exactly? I don't think I got your name..."

I narrowed my eyes at the man once more, waiting to see what he would say next. But all the man did was pick up his briefcase once more, swiftly turn on his heels, and took a step away from our table.

"If you mention my client when a dead body shows up, I will be seeing you in court."

I jumped from my seat as I watched the man head towards the door to leave the cafe as I yelled after him.

"When? You mean if? *If* a dead body shows up!" I hollered, immediately causing several heads to turn my way. It was an odd topic to be discussing over a cup of coffee, but I had seen weirder. Was currently living weirder.

"That is what I said," he replied as the bell above the door jingled and he exited the cafe.

"He one hundred percent said *when* and not *if*," Daniel chimed in as he sat at the coffee table with coffee in hand. Again, I had forgotten he was here. I dropped back into my seat as I rested my head in my hand. That man had messed up his words. Was it on purpose? I wasn't sure. It could have been a simple mistake. But we were talking about a dead body, not something minor. What was most concerning was the real estate company said they didn't have anyone in town but they had a lawyer on standby here? Something was going on, and I was leaning towards the suit-wearing man being involved.

Chapter 8

After bidding farewell to Daniel, I made my way out of the cafe with both sets of papers in hand. I had to get back to Doctor Charles and report my findings and see if she had any insights that might clear things up. It looked like the odds of Michael actually dying had been increased by the man in the suit. I grimaced at the thought. There was no way I was qualified to be delivering this type of information. With my pace quickened to the point it turned into a run, I ran down the street looking like a madwoman with papers in hand.

I screeched to a halt at the closed sign on the Cracking Chiropractor's door. I knocked on the door. My news couldn't wait. I had to tell her what I'd found out. Time was of the essence; Michael's life hung in the balance. When Doctor Charles didn't show up immediately, I banged on the door louder to make sure if she was the back she would be able to hear me. A minute later, she had emerged from the back, her eyes wide as she rushed to the door to let me in.

"Kat, please tell me you don't have bad news."

I froze as I stared at the doctor. Technically, I did have bad news, but this whole case was one bad thing after another. Her eyes dropped as her lips curved into a frown, understanding that no response had to mean I had bad news.

"Come in."

After entering the office, she locked the door and motioned me to follow her back to the exam room. It was better we talked in the back so anyone passing by wouldn't see us. Especially a suit-wearing man.

"I have some news to share with you," I started as we entered the exam room. By instinct, I made my way over to the exam table to take a seat.

"I do as well," Doctor Charles countered as I paused in retrieving the new legal document packet I had received. "The real estate company called."

"Called?" The hairs on the back of my neck stood up, as I knew exactly why they had called. After all, I had called them pretending to be someone I wasn't and now they were looking into things and handing out cease-and-desist notices.

"They have lowered their offer because of some unforeseen risks."

I scratched at the back of my neck, unease growing. *Risks* that came in the form of one Kat Jones. *Me.* I had caused the doctor to lose out on a million-dollar deal.

"Kat?" Doctor Charles asked as she must have noticed my nervousness. I felt bad that she would lose out on the chance to make a million dollars. I know if it were me, I would be crying.

"Are you going to accept the new offer?" I asked.

"I told them no, but they insisted I think it over. I just needed a bit of time." She took in a huge suck of air. "Michael doesn't have time, though."

I shuddered. She was right. Michael didn't have time, and if the suit-wearing man had his way, his time was going to run out. Regret twisted into a knot in the pit of my stomach. I was fully intent on sharing the news that I had come across, but it might just be the tipping point for the doctor. So I swallowed my tongue and kept quiet.

"Human."

From the corner of my eye, I could see the rusty orange cat, Ambrose, making its way over to me. Couldn't she tell that now wasn't the right time? Ignoring the cat, I jumped up from the exam table, grabbing my papers.

"I got to go."

I needed to get out of here before the doctor saw me talking to her cat like it could hold a conversation. That would not go over well. I might as well just tell her Michael was as good as six feet in the ground.

As I entered the waiting room, I froze, my gaze instantly locking on a man walking down the street. His black suit standing out like a sore thumb, his briefcase swung with every step. I narrowed my gaze as I crept up to the door to peer outside, but he just kept on walking.

"I'll be back, Doctor!" I called as I jerked the door open and followed after the man. Doctor Charles called out my name, no doubt wondering what information I was supposed to share with her, but that would have to wait. Time would be better spent following after this man. If he was so sure Michael would end up dead, then he had to know where he was.

With all the stealth that I could muster, which wasn't a lot, certainty nothing to rival a cat, I followed after the man who was number one on my list. I clung to the shop walls just in case he decided to have a look around and I would need to bolt. Oblivious to me stalking him, he continued down the street, never stopping to window shop. We ventured farther and farther away from Doctor Charles' practice. Mrs.

Higgins would be disappointed to know I was focusing on one suspect instead of all of them, but that slip was the biggest mess up. I couldn't help but trail behind the man to see what he was going to do next.

Just then, the man paused. I ducked against the little walkway leading to a shop, hoping he wouldn't see me. f needed, I would make a run for it, but I wanted to see what he was up to.

Please don't see me. Please don't see me...

I held my breath, waiting for him to come over and yell at me. To tell me I was stalking him, which I was, and then to say he would see me in court.

"What are you doing in my spot?"

I looked over to see a cat I wasn't familiar with looking at me.

"Are you pretending to sleep like a cat? If so, you are doing it wrong."

"You got to be kidding me!" Of course, a cat would find me. Of course they would think I was trying to mimic them.

"Get lost!" I whispered as I looked over to the suit-wearing man, only to jump up. He was on the move again! He turned and entered a shop and I crouched below the open window in hopes of hearing something useful. He reached into his pocket and pulled out a phone, clicking a single button and pressing it against his ear.

"Yes, sir ... Kat Jones..." I straightened my back at hearing my name once more. The volume in the store fluctuating making it hard to hear every word. He loved saying my name, and I wished he find a new fascination. "Kill ... understood."

Now I really hoped he found something else to fixate on. I thought having cat issues were going to be the worst thing in my life, but I had just stumbled upon something much, much worse. I gulped as I stared at the suit-wearing man nodding profusely while still on the phone. I ducked under the window and I just sat there for a moment, replaying what I just heard.

Kill...

Kat Jones...

My name and the word *kill* had been used in the same sentence. I was sure there were other words muttered, but he had spoken softer at those moments and I couldn't decipher what he said. But I had one thousand percent heard two things that should never be in the same sentence. If Michael was already six feet in the ground, he was about to have a buddy join him down there.

The unease in my stomach prevented me from waiting outside for him, because I wasn't sure if I kept following him that I would be alive for long. So I did one of the worst things possible when overhearing someone wanting to kill me.

I ran home.

Chapter 9

I covered the distance home in the blink of an eye—several blinks of the eye but still faster than normal—going as fast my legs would allow. If I had to sit down and think about it, I would much rather go out my way than his—maybe doing something I loved or even in my sleep. Anything that wasn't related to the talking cats.

I could just imagine it now, what my tombstone would say: *RIP Kat Jones. Local crime solving extraordinaire and cat whisperer.*

I shivered at that thought. Maybe having something with cats wasn't as bad as being killed. Because getting killed was not even on the list of possible ways I would want to go out. Never crossed my mind one second that was how I wanted it to happen, and I wanted to make sure it didn't come true.

Then again, I was only doing this because I was being controlled by a cat—and partially my next-door neighbor Mrs. Higgins. But mostly it was the cat's fault. I sighed. I had to figure this out, because I was too young to die.

"Cats, where are you!" I screamed as I bolted into my front door, quickly making sure to close it behind me and lock it. After popping off my shoes, I headed straight into my living room. It wasn't yet time for Lola to return home for my scheduled call with her mother, and she was absolutely making the best of it. No doubt signing me up for another case now, knowing I was well on my way to ending up six feet in the dirt before this one could be wrapped up. My shoulders sagged. What had my life come to?

"Cats...?" I called out once more as there was no pitter-patter of their soft paws as they came to greet me. One would think they would be happy to see the one who feeds them. But these were talking cats after all. They weren't normal.

"Luna? Zaira?" I called once more, projecting my voice as I listened for any source of noise that would indicate just where in my home they were. And finally I heard it. The little gray blob that was tucked between the pillows on my couch had moved and darted off. Well, I had found Zaira, and just as usual she would not be offering her services.

"You rang, human?"

"I sure did," I answered as I turned to the other gray cat with half an inch longer fur who was making her way towards me.

"You bring home more wet food?"

"Uh ... no?" I stared at the feline, who sat down at my feet, wondering why she was asking me about wet cat food. Then again, this was Luna. What else was to be expected? "Never mind the food. I need your help, Luna."

"Of course you do. It's going to cost you ... double wet food."

I smacked my head. Luna and food went hand in hand every time. "You know your mom is going to get suspicious when she sees you put on extra weight."

"Double wet food or no deal."

"I might end up dead anyway, so why not? Double wet food it is," I countered, as I reached out to pick up Luna's paw so I could shake on it.

"Dead? You should have mentioned that before the deal!"

"Funny … I was thinking Lola should have done the same," I sarcastically replied. I sat down on the floor as I got to work, bringing the gray feline up to speed. "There is this man in an all-black suit with a briefcase. I need you to keep an on eye on him and let me know if he talks to anyone weird."

"Who counts as weird?"

"Basically anyone who interacts with him. Can you do that for me? Keep an eye on him?"

"By myself?" she inquired.

I tapped my chin. Should I send her alone? Luna wasn't as graceful as Lola. Not even a fraction as sneaky as the feline that roamed outside. Not to mention Luna could easily be bribed if the right brand of wet cat food was offered. I let loose a deep sigh. No, I couldn't send Luna by herself, and Zaira had already bolted before I could ask her for help. So who could I send with her? It wasn't like I could just stroll up to Mrs. Higgins and ask her if she could go on a stakeout with my cat that she couldn't communicate with. That would only get me sent to the hospital for a possible concussion, so that meant all my neighbors were a no go.

Wait…

Not all my neighbors. There was one that could understand Luna, the one that had moved into the home across the street after it had been repaired from the vandalism.

"I found you the purr-fect partner," I answered, inserting a pun that I know would not be picked up by the cat. I just couldn't resist, it was purr-fect. It wasn't the time to be making jokes—my life was on the line after all—but if one knows death is about to come knocking, it would make anyone delirious.

"Who?"

"You will see."

I stood, making my way back over to my front door to put on my shoes. I had a cat to kidnap.

"I'll be right back!" I shouted to the felines as I closed the door behind me and swiftly made my way across the street. There was a cat on this block that was already familiar with all the antics that came with talking cats. Hopefully, they would be able to provide some help so I could live a few more years. Though the last time her and Luna had paired up, they weren't much help, but things could change. I sighed. I hope things changed, because if not, then I wasn't going to be here for long.

With Alec living across the street, it only took a moment to cross the street and up his front steps to knock on his door. I paused right before my knuckles could hit the wood. Could I just knock on his door and ask to borrow his cat? Was that a thing? If it wasn't, it was about to be, as I didn't have time to waste. With a deep sigh, I knocked on his door.

"Coming!" a lady's voice filtered through the door before there was a rustling noise, followed by the door being jerked open. On the opposite side wasn't Alec Ford, which would have made things easier, but instead his mother stood there. Mrs. Ford. With her long curly brown hair pulled up into a messy bun on her head, her glasses hanging around her neck and standing at least three heads smaller than me, she shot me a smile and ushered me inside.

"Oh, Kat! Come in!"

"Ah. It's okay. Is Alec home?"

"He should be back shortly. You are more than welcome to wait here for him."

"No. It's okay."

"Is something wrong, deary? Do you need help with something?"

There was concern dripping from her voice as she looked me up and down. No doubt putting on her motherly instincts to see if I was harmed in any way. I might not be harmed yet, but the longer I sat around, the more it was going to become a reality.

"I have a weird request ... can I borrow your cat, Dream?"

"For?" she asked as her head tilted to the side, exposing the little feline that I was trying to rope into helping me to make her way forward to stand by the door.

"Cat play date?"

"Dream has a date?" the cat chimed in.

I bit my tongue to stop myself from speaking and correcting the little fluffball that liked to talk weird. It was a time to talk to humans and not show I was crazy by having a conversation with an animal.

"Perfect idea! Why didn't I think about that? Let me just grab her supplies!"

"No, that's okay! I got a bunch of cat stuff already! Thank you, Mrs. Ford! I'll return Dream later!"

Without further ado, I crouched, scooping up the cat into my arms and hightailing it back across the street. The eyes staring into my back already let me know she thought I was an odd one. Just another name on the growing list, because *everyone* thought I was weird, and I was starting to think I was as well. How else could I explain having the ability to talk to cats?

Chapter 10

"Did you kidnap her?"

"No, Luna. I did not kidnap Dream. Her owner willingly handed her over." With the successful retrieval of Dream, I quickly put Luna in my backpack and carried the other cat in my arms as I made my way back to the last spot I saw the man who wanted to kill me. This time I was bringing reinforcements who were going to do my dirty work to make sure I stayed alive.

"Dream gets wet food as well?"

I rolled my eyes. She had overheard Luna talking nonstop about how excited she was for the extra food as I stuffed her into the backpack. I had once tried to reduce her food to put her on a diet, but Luna was Luna. If she wanted extra food, she found a way to find it.

"Why not..." I replied to Dream. "Extra wet food if you keep the man in your sights at all times."

"Maybe your life should get threatened more often if it means more food. We could always do with some extra wet food."

This time, I wised up and didn't respond. Luna was just a feline who adored food so much she was willing to sacrifice her current caregiver.

I hurried down the street to the last place I saw the man. Once I set the cats lose on their mission to stalk my killer, I would have to focus on my true mission of finding Michael. We were both on a time limit, but I was sure his time was running out faster than mine. In order to find him, I would need my own backup to make sure if the cats failed in their mission that I wasn't snuck up on the suit-wearing man. Maybe Mrs. Higgins? No, that wouldn't work. If something were to go sideways, I wouldn't want her to get involved. Mr. Higgins would never let me hear the end of it. And honestly, if it came down to it and things got out of hand. It always came down to the saying, *You don't have to outrun the killer, just the other person.* And that was something I couldn't do to Mrs. Higgins. I needed to find someone else somehow.

"Hey, Kat! You get another cat already?"

I stopped and I turned to see Daniel waving across the street. I couldn't help but smile as I watched him run to where I stood. If I was going to outrun someone, then I had no problem going against him. He instantly reached out to pet the cat in my arms. Dream let out a long string of purrs, which caused Luna to announce her presence: "What about me?"

"Walking around with two cats?" Daniel inquired as he looked over my shoulder to the head poking out my backpack. "Going to the vet?" He stopped petting Dream to give Luna the attention she wanted.

"Not quite. Still working on the case," I answered.

"Still no luck putting things together, then? So where are you going with the two cats?" he asked as he stopped giving Luna love. "Please tell me you aren't going back to the fish shop." There was mirth hidden in his tone, reminding me of what had happened when I took Luna to the fish shop for the first time and how that had ended in disaster.

One I would not be repeating in my lifetime. I wasn't sure if there was a saying about not letting a cat into a fish shop, but there should be one if it didn't exist.

"Absolutely not," I replied.

"Then where you going with these two beauties?"

Instead of answering, I opted to ask my own question, completely changing the topic: "Are you free? Do you have time to help me with something?"

"With the case again?"

I nodded my head. But I had to bring him up to speed. He wasn't there when I overheard the suit-wearing man mutter my name and *kill* in the same sentence.

"Well, you see…" I motioned for him to lean in close so I could whisper into his ear as I tucked Dream into my chest as I didn't want the world to know about someone getting killed. With my words hot against his ear, I spilled everything, getting him up to speed, omitting the part where I was going to let loose the cats in the city on a mission. That was something I couldn't explain.

"What? They are going to kill you too?" he screamed, drawing the attention of people passing by on the street. With a few weird glances shot our way, and a smile returned, I bopped Daniel on the head.

"Go ahead and proclaim it to the world, why don't you!" I whispered harshly to him.

"Sorry. I'm sorry. But that doesn't explain the cats," he said, motioning to Dream, who was still in my arms, and Luna still in the backpack. Right, of course, I was still holding the cats. I should have set them loose on their mission before engaging Daniel for his assistance, but I couldn't turn back time.

"Ah. I need to drop them off somewhere. Can you meet up with me in an hour?"

"Okay. Should I bring something? A bat? Pepper spray? Something?"

"Whatever floats your boat," I answered as I sidestepped him and continued my way down the street to the last spot I had seen the man. A part of me knew he wouldn't still be there, but a part of me hoped luck was on my side and that he would at least be somewhere nearby.

With just a simple glance into the store, I could already tell he wasn't there. Of course, luck wouldn't be on my side. It never was. Why else would it give me the ability to talk to cats? Now I would need to track him down somehow in order to get the cats on their mission.

"What are you doing?"

A scream ripped from my throat as I turned around to see who spoke to me, only to have to glance down at the orange Abyssinian cat, Ambrose, who belonged to the doctor.

"Aren't you supposed to be working my case?" she asked, and I had to roll my eyes. It was always about what the cats wanted. Did anyone care that I had a hit out on me and that I was going to end up dead? Obviously not.

"I'm working it. Things got tricky. You know, the kind of stuff that could also have me winding up dead?"

"And?"

I wanted to pull out my hair at the orange cat's indifference. I was truly just a tool to be used by these felines. Did anyone love me and see me as a human being who just wanted to live a simple life with no talking cats?

"Look, can you help Dream and Luna track down the suit-wearing man and keep an eye out on him so I can find out what's going on with your owner, okay? Can you do that for me?"

"Okay, then."

I let loose a sigh of relief as I quickly set Dream down on the ground, then I removed my backpack and let Luna hop out. Ignoring a few looks in my direction for the gathering herd of cats on the public street, I lowered myself to be closer to their height.

"A few ground rules. One: stick together. We got dumb and dumber over here. So two: Ambrose, you are in charge," I said, pointing to the orange cat, who nodded, pleased with the leadership position bestowed onto her. "And three: don't do anything Lola would do, and make sure to return to my house before nightfall. Got it?"

"Got it!" they shouted before turning and walking down the street, the three of them forcing anyone who dared to walk in their path to scurry to the side to avoid stepping on them. Luna stopped to stare into a store, only to get bopped on the head by Ambrose, and once more they walked again.

I shook my head as I turned back to go meet up with Daniel so we could start our search, already knowing it would be up to us to solve everything, as I had little faith in the ability of the three cats I had just unleashed onto the world.

Chapter 11

"What took you so long?" I inquired as Daniel came running down the street up to me. A few large items were bouncing around in his arms. When I had first spotted him, I didn't know what he was holding, but it was impossible to not know now that he was in front of me. He pulled one item out and thrust it into my face.

"A bat?"

"Yes, I figured having some protection was better than no protection."

He did have a point, as I shrugged and accepted the bat out of his hand. Instantly, I threw the weapon over my shoulder to hold on to it. The power of wielding a weapon flowed through me. Who knew it would have that type of impact instantly? I should have been walking around with this before.

"And the shovel?" I asked as I pointed to Daniel's personal choice of a weapon that was resting on his shoulder. He tilted his head as he looked at the item with a frown.

"I was thinking ... this could no longer be a rescue but a body recovery. And if there is going to be a dead body, surely it would be buried?"

I stared at Daniel. I had only been jokingly thinking about being buried six feet in the ground. It wasn't a literal statement, but maybe I should have taken it more seriously. Because of that tidbit of information, I could almost kiss Daniel, but I didn't. With the time that had passed, it might just have changed to the worst-case scenario, the one I had been trying to avoid. Michael might already be dead, and if he was, they would bury him. No way would someone just off him in the middle of town and leave him out for people to find him. Unless they were total psychos. Which could be the case, but I couldn't think like that. If they were okay doing that to Michael, they would be okay doing that to me.

"You are a genius. I knew there was another reason to bring you along, other than hoping I could outrun you."

"What?" He craned his head back to look at me, eyebrow slightly raised.

"Oh, not important." I let loose a nervous laugh. I had done it again, letting a tidbit of information slip when I shouldn't have. "What is important is that if they are going to kill Michael, they are going to bury him. The time is already ticking down, so there is a good chance Michael is already where they plan to kill him. So where would that be?"

"In the woods. But what part of town would be best to do it?"

"Not the park, too easy for people to accidentally stumble upon them," I answered.

"What do they do in the movies?" Daniel asked.

"Either bury them in their back yard or drive them out of town."

"Does anyone have forests in their back yards?"

My mouth dropped as I stared at Daniel. Did anyone have a forest in their back yard? There was one neighborhood that had direct access to the forest area that had been left not yet logged for more homes to be built. People didn't venture into it because there was nothing of great value to see. No hidden waterfall to enjoy, not even a cleared path for people to take to explore. I knew that for a fact because I had to venture into those woods one time in order to locate a missing cat, one that was building an army in the woods for who knows what.

If I had to guess ... world domination.

"My back yard..." I whispered as I thought it over some more. We would be taking a huge risk by going out exploring the woodsy area to see if we could find anything that would allow us to find our kidnapped person. But I didn't know the area too well. It would be hard to search it without getting absolutely lost and wasting time. We needed a guide, but who? As I thought over everyone who lived in our neighborhood, I crossed out name after name till I just had one name left. The cat building an army for when she decided to take on the world.

Lola.

"Come! I might know who to ask if there has been anything going on in the woods behind my home."

"Does someone live behind your house?" Daniel asked as he followed me down the street. We strode forward with extra pep in our step in hopes of covering the distance faster.

"In a sense. Sure."

We spent the rest of the trip in silence, ignoring the people passing who had to be questioning why we were walking around with a bat and a shovel. Just two crazy people in a crazy town trying to find a crazy person before they committed a murder. That sounded absolutely not normal. I glanced to Daniel, who had his face morphed into one of focus, his shovel bobbing on his shoulder. I knew for a fact that we stuck out like a sore thumb. Good thing the three cats had already scurried off or it would have been an even more ridiculous scene to see the three of them trailing behind us.

"So what happens if we find Michael?" Daniel asked as we rounded the corner to my street.

"Honestly, I don't know."

I never thought about what happened when we found Michael. It was always just *beat the clock*, find Michael, and that solves my case. But there was a good chance that by finding Michael we were going to stumble upon two different scenes. The first would have Michael still alive but near his kidnapper because they are about to kill him. Or Michael would be dead and no one would be in sight. Both sounded absolutely horrible, and I couldn't wait to wash my hands of this mess so I didn't have to think about it anymore.

"Good thing you brought a bat and shovel. We will just have to wait and see," I exclaimed as we reached my house.

Instead of going into my home, I headed around my house, walking through my small back yard that wasn't fenced in, and into the forest that surrounded my block. Instantly the sun disappeared, only providing a few rays of light whenever it happened to break through the canopy of the trees.

"You didn't happen to bring a flashlight too? Just in case."

"Ah no," Daniel said, as I felt him brush against my side, standing close with his shovel armed in his hands. As I paused to take a look at the man beside me, I realized there was a slight shake in his arms.

"Are you scared?"

"I got lost in the forest once during a camping trip. I'm not a big fan."

I pursed my lips but continued deeper into the woods, recalling the last place that I had seen Lola to see if she was still around so I could inquire if there had been anything odd unfolding in these woods other than her building an army in my back yard. That was a separate issue, one that I wouldn't concern myself with unless it somehow ended up on my front door, literally. Until then, it could stay out of sight so it would be out of mind.

"If you see a cat, let me know."

"Going to rescue it at a time like this?"

"Absolutely not, but they could lead us to where we need to go."

"Cats aren't the same as dogs."

I snorted at Daniel. He didn't have to tell me twice that cats and dogs were vastly different.

I couldn't help but wonder how the other three felines were doing with the task I had assigned them. Had they been able to find the lawyer walking around in a suit or had they got distracted? With Luna, that was possible, but I had to place my faith in the orange cat and hope she kept the other two in line.

Chapter 12

We continued our trek through the forest. One of us was armed with a bat and the other was armed with a shovel. Two odd people embarking into the unknown.

"Did you hear that?" Daniel whispered as he jumped forward, almost slamming into me, gripping onto my arm. His fingers dug into my skin as he held on for dear life.

"Hear what?" I answered back, keeping my voice low as well as I tried to pry his hand off of me. I hadn't heard anything, but that didn't mean there wasn't anything out there. No reason to be loud and tip off whoever might be out there that could potentially be lurking about. But the hair on the back of my neck stood on edge as I took a cautious step forward. We couldn't wait around to see exactly what Daniel had heard or we would be stuck here when it got dark. And that was absolutely not going to happen.

"Maybe it was nothing..." Daniel muttered as he finally let go of me.

"We should pick up the pace. Once it gets dark I'm hightailing it out of here."

The trees grew thicker the more we walked away from my home. With every step, we had to be careful not to stumble on the exposed roots and the random junk that was scattered about. Already we had passed several tires, a pile of cans, and a shopping cart. There was something going on in the forest that involved human activity and I didn't want to run into anybody. I clutched on to my bat tighter.

"Wait!" Daniel hissed. "Please tell me you heard that?" he urgently whispered as he gripped onto me once more, his fingers digging into my skin as he moved his head on a swivel, trying to locate whatever he was hearing. I looked around, trying to see what he may have been looking at, but nothing was standing out. All there was nature, junk, and two humans, who were us. At this rate, I was starting to think that Michael might not actually be out here.

"Daniel, nothing is out there," I replied.

"No! I'm sure I heard something."

"It might just be us."

"I don't think. Ack!"

A high, piercing scream erupted from the man as he let me go in order to throw his shovel at a tree. It twirled in the air before banging against a tree and clattering to the ground. I held my breath, waiting for whatever Daniel had noticed to come out. Nothing happened. I gulped, hoping Daniel was just going crazy and that we weren't being followed. A shiver coursed through my body. Could it be the suit-wearing man who was trying to kill me?

"It looks like it's nothing. Daniel, go get your shovel," I whispered softly, jabbing my elbow into Daniel's side. I wasn't going to be the one to go retrieve his item, just in case there was something behind that tree.

"I'm sure I saw something!"

There was only one safe way to figure out if someone was truly behind the tree.

"Come out!" I yelled to the spot where the shovel lay on the ground. Maybe it would be a squirrel? Or a dog that accidentally got loose?

"Well, are you going to throw something at me again?" an annoyed voice piped up from behind the tree. Instantly, I loosened my hold on my bat as I sighed. It wasn't a squirrel, nor a dog.

It was just a cat.

"Lola," I said as I rubbed my temples when the hidden figure finally exposed herself.

"You knew it was your cat from its meow?"

I tossed a look over my shoulder to peer at Daniel. Of course he couldn't hear Lola talk. All of it just sounded like a cat meowing. But could I tell cats apart from their meow? Absolutely not. I wasn't much of a cat person. There had to be owners out there who could, but I wasn't one.

"Wait right here." I motioned to Daniel to stay put as I quickly made my way over to the tree, scooping up Lola in the process, who let out an annoyed grunt at being picked up randomly. When we were safely behind the tree and out of view of Daniel, I set her down on the ground.

"What are you doing out here?"

"The real question is, what are you doing out here when you have a case?" she countered.

"I'm working the case." I rolled my eyes at the fact that was the first thing she thought of. "Have you seen anyone suspicious out here?"

"Of course I have."

"Like humans are out and about in the woods?" I clarified, hoping she would have useful information.

"Of course."

"Can you lead us to where you saw the humans?"

"I suppose."

"Lola, you could sound a little more enthusiastic, you know. I am working this because of the cats." And humans. But I left that out.

"Well, let's wrap this up so you can start working on the next one!" She gave me an enthusiastic reply as she maneuvered out from behind the tree.

"Wait..." I paused as I watched her. "What?" I called as I followed after the feline that like to cause me headaches. There was no way Lola had signed me up for another case! She didn't wait for me to tell her how horrible this was becoming. There was someone out there who wanted me dead! They weren't just looking to scare me—no they wanted me six feet in the ground, and I don't think Lola understood how nerve-racking that could be.

"What were you doing behind the tree?" Daniel asked as he approached, picking up the shovel in the process as he got closer.

"Follow the cat. It will take us to other humans that have been in the forest."

Daniel let out a chuckle as he slung the shovel over his shoulder. "You must really be a cat whisperer."

I'm glad that was all he said, and he didn't question my weird behavior that always seemed to come out when I was near cats. Lola didn't wait around for me to explain things to Daniel, for she had already started making her way through the foliage to wherever she had seen the humans. Hopefully, we would be able to solve this case and put everything to rest.

Chapter 13

L ola sprinted through the woods, not caring for one moment that we were human and not as nimble as she, or that it would take us a moment longer to get our footing and not prance around like we were light as a feather.

"Are you sure we should be following the cat?" Daniel asked as he was only a few paces behind me. I didn't respond right away. Lola was all we had. His insight had brought us to the forest, and the information from Lola would bring us to the humans we were hunting. That is, if they were the same people we were looking for; that had yet to be determined, but we were about to find out very soon—if we ever made it to wherever Lola was taking us.

I bit my tongue, preventing myself from calling out to the feline to make sure we were going the right way—that she was indeed going to provide something useful and wasn't just going to be leading us on a wild goose chase.

But she slowed her pace to just a trot as she tossed a look in my direction.

"Up ahead in the shed!" she exclaimed, which had to sound like pointless meows to Daniel. He was the lucky one, not having the ability to communicate to cats. I would be very happy to switch places with him.

A rundown wooden shack popped into view as we got closer to where Lola was taking us.

"Humans were in there."

"Thanks, Lola," I whispered as I came to a halt, hiding behind a tree, unsure if we were the only humans lurking in the woods. Daniel came to a rest next to me, knowing to hide behind the tree to scope out the area.

"Quick, look around to see if anything stands out. Then we leave, okay?"

I made sure to keep my voice low.

"Of course. In and out," Daniel whispered. "I got your back."

It would be better if he would go first, but that would be a hard sell. He had come out here with me into the woods and that would have to be enough for the moment. So, with a deep breath, I pressed forward, inching my way past the trees toward the shack, clutching on to the bat tighter and tighter with every step I took. My stomach was rolling, my body tensing, as we finally reached the door.

"Is the cat coming?" Daniel asked as I turned towards where Lola was sitting. Of course she wasn't coming. She was content with sending the humans into danger, and not getting her paws dirty. But what was I supposed to expect? This was my fourth case and the saltiness I had towards her was starting to die down a little; it was starting to become expected.

The door to the shack was closed, but there were cracks in the wood that would allow someone to peek through to see if there was anything inside. I crept closer, both hands gripping the bat tightly, ready to swing at anything that moved my way. With both eyes wide open, I peered into the hole to see that it looked like it was used for storage. But who would be using this place out here in the middle of the woods to store things? The first thought that crossed my mind was that had to be used for something illegal and now we had stumbled upon it and were about to put our prints all over the place. I had seen enough cop shows to know what happens. But I pushed the thought aside. I couldn't be thinking about a made-up situation when I had a very real situation on my hands. Michael was missing, and someone had threatened to kill me. Who cares if my prints were on something? At least if I wound up dead, it would provide some clues.

I scanned the shed, trying to see if there was anything that stood out or if I could hear something breathing in there. But there was no noise other than my heart pounding against my chest.

"Should we go in?" Daniel asked softly as he tried to peer over me to look into the shed. It was now or never, so I nodded, and with a long exhale pushed the door open with my bat. Just as I had expected, the wooden door expelled a loud creak as it slowly swung open. There was no scatter of dust, which meant this place was visited often enough that dust couldn't build up. I gulped as I pointed my bat inside, swinging it around to see if I struck anything. But I didn't. Pleased that I wasn't going to run into anything upon entry, I entered the shed. With the bat gripped tightly, I scanned to see if anything else was going to pop out but nothing yet.

"Is it safe to come in?"

I turned towards the door. Daniel was still standing outside.

"Yeah, you can come in."

With his own shovel held tight, he walked slowly into the shed, his eyes wide as he took everything in. I didn't take Daniel to be someone who scared easily, especially with his cool aura at the cafe. But I understand his position. It wasn't every day someone had to go exploring the woods for a person who had been kidnapped. I would have much preferred to stay home, watch TV, and forgot that the outside world existed.

"Let's hurry up and see if we can find anything," I muttered as I made my way to the back of the shed. It wasn't big, just the size of a medium walk-in closet. I didn't dare take my hands off my bat though as I used it to poke and prod the items scattered about. A few boxes sat on the ground underneath a table. Nothing jumped out, and while it would have been best to search the boxes thoroughly by removing each and every item, it wasn't going to do me much help. I wasn't even sure what I was looking for other than Michael, and he didn't fit in the boxes. The boxes were tucked underneath a workbench that had several tools scattered atop. It all contained a fair amount of rust, but nothing looked like it had blood. That was good.

The air rushed out my body as I was slammed into the workbench. My bat clattered to the ground as I gripped the edge of the table to try to get my bearings underneath me.

"What?" I groaned as I looked over my shoulder to see a mop of brown hair.

"Daniel?"

"B-b-b-b-bones!" Daniel screamed as he pointed to the corner of the shed that was hidden behind the door when we had opened it.

"What?"

"Bones! There are bones over there! Oh, my gosh, he is dead!" he hollered as he tried to push away from the bones in the corner. As I maneuvered around him to get a better look at what caused him to scream, there were indeed bones on the ground.

"No way... you got to be kidding me."

Reality was sinking in at the realization that we were too late for Michael. And if we were too late for him, was it too late for me?

"We have to get out of here!" I exclaimed as I bent to pick up my bat. There was no way I was trekking back through the forest without my weapon by my side.

"Where are you going?" said a voice.

A scream ripped through my throat as I bumped my head on the workbench.

"It's just your cat." Daniel said as he pointed to Lola in the doorway. Daniel had only heard the meow, so he wasn't startled by the extra voice that had joined us. A curse of being able to understand cats.

"Why are you guys screaming in here?"

I shot Lola a look as if to tell her *not now*. I couldn't talk to her with Daniel around. Things were tense as it is, and I didn't need him to start thinking I was going crazy and could understand my cat.

"What do we do about the bones?" he asked as we carefully made our way to the front of the shed to leave.

"Leave it. We will tell the cops," I replied.

"You screamed over fake bones?" Lola inquired as she poked at the pile in the corner before picking one of up in her mouth.

"Oh, I think I'm going to be sick."

The dry heave from Daniel was enough to excuse himself as he ran out of the shed back outside, giving me the perfect opportunity to talk to Lola alone.

"Fake bones? They aren't real?"

"Of course not."

"Why would there be fake bones out here in the middle of the woods?"

"Don't know. Humans have weird habits," Lola responded as she sat down next to the pile of fake bones. Now that I was looking at them, they looked awfully pristine, almost like they had a polish to them. Hesitantly, I reached out and picked up a bone to inspect it. It was awfully light, and felt plastic. So they were fake.

"You get your cat to stop eating the bones?" Daniel asked as his head popped around the door to peer at me. His eyes grew wide.

"What are you doing?" he whispered as he pointed to the bone in my hand.

"It's fake."

"It is?" He finally reentered the shed and stepped closer. "Huh, look at that. Who would have thought?" Daniel poked at a different piece that was in the pile before gaining the courage to pick up one up to examine. "Yep, it's fake."

"Exactly, what are fake bones doing out here? And where is Michael? Did we guess wrong and use up all our time?"

Chapter 14

"Maybe it was just some teenagers?" Daniel asked as he placed the bone back on the ground. I followed suit, placing my own that I picked up to inspect back in the pile, doing my best to put it back exactly how I found it so as not to alert whoever this shed and alarm them. While the bones weren't real, we still didn't know what was going on.

"Let's go before it gets dark." I stood from crouching to inspect the pile, dusting off my knees.

"Wait, do you hear that?"

"Hear what, Daniel?" I inquired as I picked up my bat to swing over my shoulder.

"Surely you heard that?" He looked out of the shed door.

"Maybe it's another cat?" I asked as I too poked my head out to see if I could see what had spooked Daniel. Not that it took a lot to spook him, I was finding out. He was just as easily spooked as I was. The only difference was that he had way better hearing than me.

"I don't hear anything. Let's go before something does pop up."

I attempted to leave, but Daniel gripped me tightly.

"Something is out there. Trust me. I got good ears, kind of have to when you need to take orders when the cafe gets loud."

I bit my lip. It wasn't that I didn't trust Daniel's instincts. He had very good instincts that led us to the forest in the first place. Without him, I don't think I would have made the connection to search out here. I would still have been walking around town snooping around the suit-wearing man instead of focusing on finding Michael. But we couldn't wait around here all day; the sunlight would soon leave, and that would force us to walk back in the dark. There was no way I would be caught dead in the forest at night, especially in a creepy shed that held fake bones.

"Shhh," Daniel urged, and I was about to retort that I hadn't said anything when I finally heard what he did. There was something out there. Someone, to be precise, for I could hear them talking. I cast a look in Daniel's direction, seeing his eyes wide. At least it wasn't another cat. But there was a sinking feeling in my stomach. I would have much preferred to encounter another talking cat in the woods than a human. If there was a human out here and their voice was getting louder, it meant they were coming here where Daniel and I still stood in the shed.

"We need to hide," I whispered harshly as I scanned the shed, trying to find a hiding spot.

"Where? There is nothing here!"

I groaned. Daniel was correct; there was nothing here to hide behind or in. We could hide under the storage bench but we would still be exposed; there was no small closet or tarps to hide us from view, just scattered tools and boxes. And I wasn't nimble enough or crazy enough to try to fold my body into a box.

"Yes, sweetie! My plan is almost complete, and then I'll take you on a world trip," a voice said, one that wasn't coming from inside the shed, which meant it was the person outside.

"What plan?" Daniel asked.

"If connected to what I think, then the kidnapping, but *shhh* ... before he hears us." I brought my finger up to my lips to silence Daniel before he started asking more questions which would expose us.

"No, she hasn't agreed to the deal yet. I don't know what is taking her so long."

The deal that popped into my mind was the deal to the doctor for her to sell her practice. With every word the man outside muttered, the more likely it was showing he was connected to Michael's kidnapping.

"I know! I thought she cared for me, but I guess not if she is holding out this long. I thought I had sweetened her up enough."

"*Me?*" I whispered to Daniel, who shrugged his shoulders. He had no clue what was going on. While I had given him the rundown of what had happened before we walked out into the woods, it was easy to focus on the parts that directly mentioned kidnapping and murder.

"Hmmm ... I thought I had made such a good impression on her. All the late nights bonding together."

What was this man going on about? He knew the doctor personally? Something wasn't adding up.

"To think, I put up working with her for so long."

Working with *her?*

The gears in my mind worked overtime as I put the pieces together. The doctor worked alone other than the one employee ... who had been kidnapped.

"I think that's Michael," I said to Daniel, who jerked his head in my direction.

"What? Isn't he supposed to be kidnapped?" Daniel exclaimed, a little too loud for comfort.

I froze, Daniel catching his own mistake as he too froze. We stared at each other, waiting for the other shoe to drop.

"Who is out there?" the man who I suspected was Michael called from outside. That was the moment everything became chaotic in the shed. I scrambled away from the door, Daniel scooting away as well, as we both looked for a way out that wouldn't involve us running into the man outside. My breathing grew heavy. I looked to Daniel. His knuckles were going white from how tight he was clutching the shovel in his hands.

One...

I mouthed to him.

Two...

Three...

And with that, we unleashed a battle cry, jerking the shed door open and bolting out into the woods. I swung wildly with my bat, trying to make myself seem crazy so the guy we supposed was Michael would be dazed and thrown off balance. It must have worked, for I saw him dart to the side and out of my way as I continued hacking at the air. I threw the bat over my shoulder and picked up speed, ready to run the whole way home and out the woods, when a high-pitched girly scream ripped through the air.

Daniel...

I paused for a moment, debating on what to do. I had joked the whole reason I'd brought Daniel with me into the woods was because, if it came down to it, I would be willing to outrun him. But now the moment had come and I couldn't bring myself to leave him. He had willingly stepped into danger to help me. I couldn't leave him out here. So against all rational thought that it would be better for someone to run for help, I turned back towards the shed, raised my bat once more, and let out a battle cry.

"Hold on, Daniel! Here I come!"

Chapter 15

I sped back through the trees towards the shed to where I had last seen Daniel. It only took a moment to see that he hadn't made it far. The man that I assumed was Michael had a hood covering his head. He had managed to tackle Daniel to the ground, and the only thing keeping the two apart was the shovel Michael had managed to thrust into the chest of his attacker. I could already see the quiver starting in his arms, and the wild look on his face at being pinned down. I knew it was the smart choice to come back for Daniel.

Mustering all the strength in my body, channeling on the craziness I knew it contained, I swung my bat like the true crazy person I was starting to become thanks to my exposure to the cats. Wildly, without a true destination in mind, only knowing I needed to get the guy off Daniel, my strike struck true. It connected with the guy's side, sending him tumbling. The attacker reached down, gripping his stomach as he let loose an anguished yell.

"Get up!" I screamed at Daniel as I kept my bat pointed out in front of me, ready to unleash all the crazy out into the world once more. Daniel, though, had a different thought on his mind. He took his shovel and swung at the guy, instantly knocking him out. He then poked the downed man with his shovel, and when the man didn't respond, he let out a triumphant cry.

"That's for tackling me!"

"Good job," I croaked as I bent down to pull down the hood so I can see who our attacker was. Recognition instantly clicked.

"It's Michael."

"Isn't he supposed to be kidnapped?" Daniel countered, as he crept a little closer to get a good look at the man.

"I thought so."

"So what is he doing walking around?"

"I'm guessing he was in on it."

"What about the guy who wanted to kill you?"

"Probably working together. Let's get out of here and get help before he wakes up."

"Don't need to tell me twice," Daniel said as he threw his shovel over his shoulder and headed off towards my house. I wasted no time at all following suit. I wanted to get out of here as soon as possible. We needed to get the police involved so they could pick up Michael. I wasn't equipped to handle prisoners; that was a murky area I'd rather not step in. Just imagining trying to explain to the police when they did eventually come around why I had a man knocked out in a shed wasn't going to go down well, even if my intentions were pure.

The walk back through the forest went by quicker than the walk in. Maybe it was due to the extra shot of adrenaline pumping through my body. When the trees broke apart and the back of my home became visible, I let out an audible whoop at managing to escape the forest in one piece.

"Kat! Is that you?" Mrs. Higgins called out as she appeared in my back yard, her gray hair pulled back into a bun, exposing the worried expression on her face. Right behind her was Mr. Higgins, who looked like he had been dragged outside without having his cup of coffee, his lips pressed together in a frown as he grumbled underneath his breath as we got closer. But it wasn't just Mr. Higgins that was behind her, for there was also Detective Davidson.

"What is going on?" I asked as I loosened my hold on my bat, staring at the people who had all gathered together for some reason.

"Your cat showed up at my house. I thought something happened to you and she got out."

"Cat?"

"The gray one."

There were two gray ones. And one had refused to help me by scurrying off and hiding in the house. The other one? I had unleashed into the world and she had somehow made it over to Mrs. Higgins' home.

She gave a look to her husband before sliding her way closer to me.

"Did you solve the case?" she whispered into my ear.

"Ah ... sort of ... I think?" I replied. I had figured out Michael had not been kidnapped, but there were still a few missing pieces.

"Kat, would you like to explain why you are holding a bat and Daniel is holding a shovel? What exactly were you doing in the woods to warrant such items?" Detective Davidson asked as he reached into the shirt pocket of his uniform to pull out his little notebook, grabbing a pen that hung on the pocket, clicking it and waiting for me to provide some type of reply.

"Well, you see ... this could all be better explained after you go get the guy knocked out in the woods."

"Guy knocked out in the woods? Let me guess, that is why you have the bat. But the shovel? Were you planning on burying him as well?" Detective Davidson inquired as he scribbled away in his notebook. "And where exactly is this guy and why is he knocked out?" he further questioned.

"He tackled me so we knocked him out," Daniel chimed in, thrusting his shovel out in a proud manner at what had unfolded in the woods.

"I'm still not understanding. Are you saying you were jumped in the woods?"

"Not exactly," I finally said, cutting Daniel off from providing any more information. "Michael..." I started as I turned to Mrs. Higgins. "...wasn't kidnapped, but seemed to have staged it all."

"Someone was kidnapped and I'm just now finding out about it?" Detective Davidson exclaimed in surprise.

"Now-now, we were going to tell you eventually."

"We? You were a part of it? Why am I not surprised?" Mr. Higgins cut in as he shot his wife a dirty look. He never liked it when she got involved in the crime in town. I agreed with him. If I could avoid crime, I would. But it was attracted to me just as much as talking cats were. I couldn't get rid of the crime-solving till I got rid of being able to communicate with cats.

"So, is anyone going to go pick him up before he wakes up?"

I broke the silence and Detective Davidson clicked his pen, flipped his notebook closed, and shoved both in his pocket before grumbling and marching off into the woods.

I hoped he knew where to go.

Chapter 16

Detective Davidson had no problem retrieving the body of Michael out from the woods, especially since I sent Daniel to go with him. There was no way I was stepping back into the area behind my home any time soon.

We were all in the police room. For some reason I had to turn in my bat but Daniel got away with still holding his shovel. "So explain this again. You wanted to solve a kidnapping case on your own?" Detective Davidson asked as I sat at the table. Michael had finally awoken, and he too sat at the table, though he had a giant red welt on his forehead thanks to the shovel Daniel liked to carry around and was still carrying.

"I didn't want to solve it. I was asked to."

"And you thought not going to the police when you were asked was the best idea?"

"You know ... that should probably be directed to someone else not me. It wasn't like I just happened upon this case. But that is beside the point! What matters is Michael was supposed to be kidnapped but he isn't. What is that about, huh, Michael?" I asked, directing my question to the man who sat with his head tilted down.

"Kat, I will be doing the questioning. I'm the detective here."

"Oh right. Sorry."

"Michael, if you please..."

The door to the room slammed open and a figure dressed all in black strolled in, the only person in town to be walking around with a suit. I jumped out of my seat, pointing a finger at him as I yelled out.

"You!"

"Hello again, Kat Jones."

"What are you doing here?"

"Representing my client." He strolled over to where Michael sat and set his briefcase on the table before looking at Detective Davidson.

"So something is going on..." he muttered as he scribbled away in his notebook that he had pulled out of his pocket earlier and set on the table

"You wanted to kill me!" I hollered, refusing to sit down back at the table. It was one thing to sit next to Michael, who had kidnapped himself and jumped Daniel. But this guy? He used my name and the word *kill* in the same sentence; he was planning to put me six feet in the ground.

"I had no such intention."

"Then why did you say my name and *kill* together? Like you were putting out a hit on me?" I inquired, my voice raising slightly. The confidence of being in the police station and in front of Detective Davidson gave me an air of comfort that I didn't have previously.

"I was speaking to my contact about and how they should kill the deal. Not kill *you*. Can we get to the real reason we are here?"

"Oh," I muttered as I sat back down in my chair. That would made sense. There had been a few words I wasn't able to hear for being outside, but now that he spoke what he had truly said, it was a lot more plausible than him trying to kill me.

"Wait ... you are representing the real estate company, but you are here representing Michael?"

"Yes," he replied curtly, not elaborating on how exactly he got to be Michael's lawyer. Good thing Detective Davidson had access to people's information. He picked up the stack of papers on the table before reading out that Michael was actually the son of the owner of the real estate company. This tidbit of information caused him to let out a tsk, as he still refused to open his mouth. I stared at Michael, trying to piece the pieces together.

"You got the doctor to pay off your loan. But did you even have a loan if your family has money?" I thought out loud. "And then you planned your kidnapping to try and get more money out of the doctor, but she didn't have it ... so you were going to have your dad pay for the company so the doctor can give you the money to save your life. Am I right?"

"Michael, is this true? Your dad will not be pleased," the lawyer chimed in as he opened his briefcase to pull out a phone.

"Don't call him!" Michael yelled before turning his heated gaze on me. "Shut up! Stop talking! You ruined everything!"

"Ruined? You tried to kill us!" Daniel exclaimed, shaking his shovel to remind him exactly of what had unfolded in the woods.

"Then you should have stayed out of it! I almost had the money. I was so close ... so close, and you had to come along and ruin it!"

"Wow..." I muttered as I leaned back in my chair. "I did it ... I solved it."

"Well, Michael, you might want to be careful with what you say. You are going to make your lawyer's job really hard."

"I'm actually not his lawyer anymore. I serve his dad, and if he was going to steal from my employer, well, that cuts my obligation to represent you." With those words, the lawyer picked up his briefcase and left the room. Just in time, as Michael let out an anguished scream.

"Well, Kat, you should head out as well before things get ugly."

"Yeah … no problem," I answered as I stood. Daniel, already making his way to the door, pulled it open, waiting for me to leave first. Just like in the woods, he had my back.

"And, Kat … you would make a mighty fine detective, but stop solving cases on your own."

I scrunched up my face. It wasn't like I wanted to solve cases in my free time.

"Well, tell the cats that!" I hollered as I stepped out into the hallway.

"Cats?" Daniel asked as he walked in step with me.

"Never mind … it's not important."

Thank you for reading Abyssinian Arrangement, if you enjoyed it please leave a review!

You can find the next book Ragdoll Ripoff here:

https://www.irisleigh.com/home/cat-aunt-cozy-mystery/

Iris Leigh

Iris Leigh stumbled upon the genre of cozy mystery by accident. Since Iris is easily scared she does her best to avoid horror books, tv shows, and films. But dying for some type of mystery without all the suspense to make her heart burst from terror was when someone asked if she had ever read a cozy mystery. Now she has fallen in love with the genre and started to write to bring her stories to life.

If you want to stay in contact with Iris and learn about upcoming releases, make sure to sign up for the newsletter! You can sign up by navigating to her website!
Website: www.irisleigh.com

Ragdoll Ripoff

A cat may be at the center of a break-in at the library.

I'm Kat Jones and my very first client needs my help to find the person responsible for swapping an ancient book with a fake. As if that isn't baffling enough; where they found the fake is a place no one knew existed.

To solve this case, I'll need to team up with Rusty. What we discover is a treasure trove of secrets that lead to the origin of the book and not who but what four-legged creature may be responsible.

https://www.irisleigh.com/home/cat-aunt-cozy-mystery/

9 781956 732108